THE
Gardener

A TRUMPET CLUB SPECIAL EDITION

August 27, 1935

Dear Uncle Jim,

Grandma told us after supper that you want me to come to the city and live with you until things get better. Did she tell you that Papa has been out of work for a long time, and no one asks Mama to make dresses anymore?

We all cried, even Papa. But then Mama made us laugh with her stories about your chasing her up trees when you were both little. Did you really do that?

I'm small, but strong, and I'll help you all I can. However, Grandma said to finish my schoolwork before doing anything else.

Your niece,
Lydia Grace Finch

September 3, 1935

Dear Uncle Jim,

   I'm mailing this from the train station. I forgot to tell you in the last letter *three important things* that I'm too shy to say to your face:

   1. I know a lot about gardening, but nothing about baking.

   2. I'm anxious to learn to bake, but is there any place to plant seeds?

   3. I like to be called "Lydia Grace"— just like Grandma.

                    Your niece,
                    Lydia Grace Finch

On the train
September 4, 1935
Dear Mama,

I feel so pretty in your dress that you made over for me. I hope you don't miss it too much.

Dear Papa,

I haven't forgotten what you said about recognizing Uncle Jim: "Just look for Mama's face with a big nose and a mustache!" I promise not to tell him. (Does he have a sense of humor?)

And, dearest Grandma,

Thank you for the seeds. The train is rocking me to sleep, and every time I doze off, I dream of gardens.

Love to all,
Lydia Grace

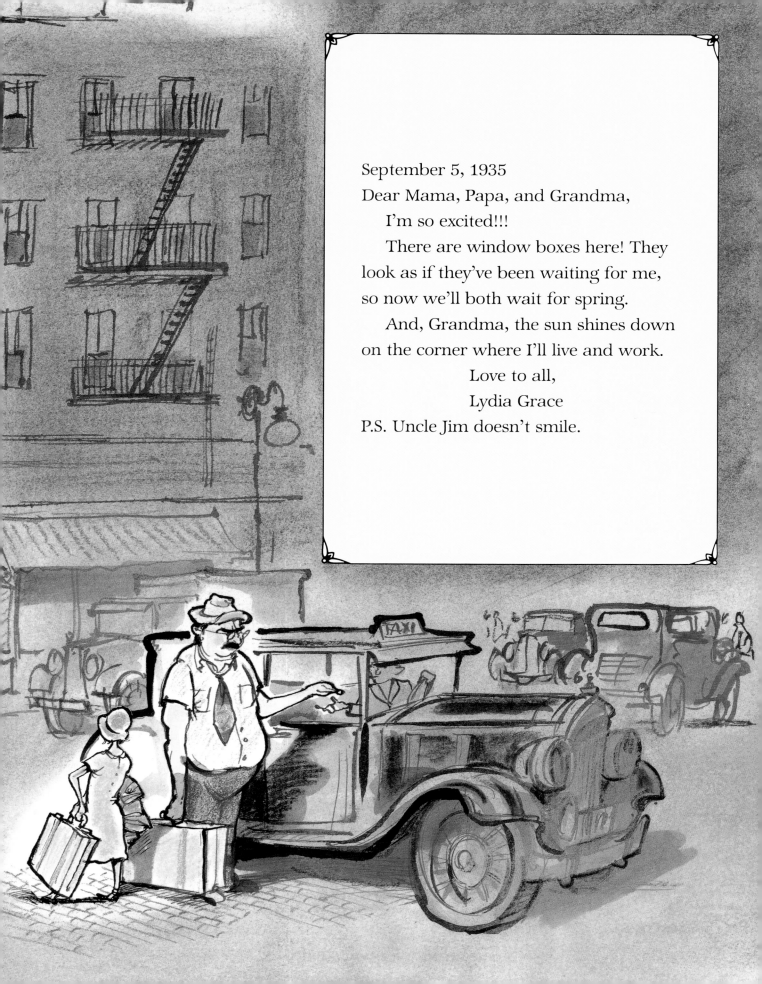

September 5, 1935
Dear Mama, Papa, and Grandma,
    I'm so excited!!!
    There are window boxes here! They look as if they've been waiting for me, so now we'll both wait for spring.
    And, Grandma, the sun shines down on the corner where I'll live and work.
            Love to all,
            Lydia Grace
P.S. Uncle Jim doesn't smile.

December 25, 1935

Dear Mama, Papa, and Grandma,

I adore the seed catalogues you sent for Christmas. And, Grandma, thank you for all the bulbs. I hope you received my drawings.

I wrote a long poem for Uncle Jim. He didn't smile, but I think he liked it. He read it aloud, then put it in his shirt pocket and patted it.

Love to all,

Lydia Grace

February 12, 1936

Dearest Grandma,

Thank you again for those bulbs you sent at Christmas. You should see them now!

I really like Ed and Emma Beech, Uncle Jim's friends who work here. When I first arrived, Emma told me she'd show me how to knead bread if I would teach her the Latin names of all the flowers I know. Now, just half a year later, I'm kneading bread and she's speaking Latin!

More good news: We have a store cat named Otis who at this very moment is sleeping at the foot of *my* bed.

Love to all,
Lydia Grace

P.S. Uncle Jim isn't smiling yet, but I'm hoping for a smile soon.

March 5, 1936

Dear Mama, Papa, and Grandma,

I've discovered a secret place. You can't imagine how wonderful it is. No one else knows about it but Otis.

I have great plans.

Thank you for all the letters. I'll try to write more, but I'm really busy planting all your seeds in cracked teacups and bent cake pans! And, Grandma, you should smell the good dirt I'm bringing home from the vacant lot down the street.

Love to all,

Lydia Grace

April 27, 1936
Dearest Grandma,

   All the seeds and roots are sprouting. I can hear you saying, "April showers bring May flowers."

   Emma and I are sprucing up the bakery and I'm playing a great trick on Uncle Jim. He sees me reading my mail, planting seeds in the window boxes, going to school, doing my homework, sweeping the floor. But he never sees me working in my secret place.

                   Love to all,
                   Lydia Grace

P.S. I'm planning on a big smile from Uncle Jim in the near future.

May 27, 1936

Dear Mama, Papa, and Grandma,

    You should have heard Emma laugh today when I opened your letter and dirt fell out onto the sidewalk! Thank you for all the baby plants. They survived the trip in the big envelope.

    More about Emma: She's helping me with the secret place. Hurrah!

                   Love to all,
                   Lydia Grace

P.S. I saw Uncle Jim almost smile today. The store was full (well, *almost* full) of customers.

June 27, 1936

Dear Grandma,

   Flowers are blooming all over the place. I'm also growing radishes, onions, and three kinds of lettuce in the window boxes.

   Some neighbors have brought containers for me to fill with flowers, and a few customers even gave me plants from their gardens this spring! They don't call me "Lydia Grace" anymore. They call me "the gardener."

                    Love to all,
                    Lydia Grace

P.S. I'm sure Uncle Jim will smile soon. I'm almost ready to show him the secret place.

July 4, 1936

Dearest Mama, Papa, and Grandma,

I am bursting with happiness! The entire city seems so beautiful, especially this morning.

The secret place is ready for Uncle Jim. At noon, the store will close for the holiday, and then we'll bring him up to the roof.

I've tried to remember everything you ever taught me about beauty.

Love to all,

Lydia Grace

P.S. I can already imagine Uncle Jim's smile.

July 11, 1936

Dear Mama, Papa, and Grandma,

    My heart is pounding so hard I'm sure the customers can hear it downstairs!

    At lunch today, Uncle Jim put the "Closed" sign on the door and told Ed and Emma and me to go upstairs and wait. He appeared with the most amazing cake I've ever seen—covered in flowers!

    I truly believe that cake equals one thousand smiles.

    And then he took your letter out of his pocket with the news of Papa's job!

I'M COMING HOME!

        Love to all, and see you soon,
        Lydia Grace

P.S. Grandma, I've given all of my plants to Emma. I can't wait to help you in your garden again. We gardeners never retire.

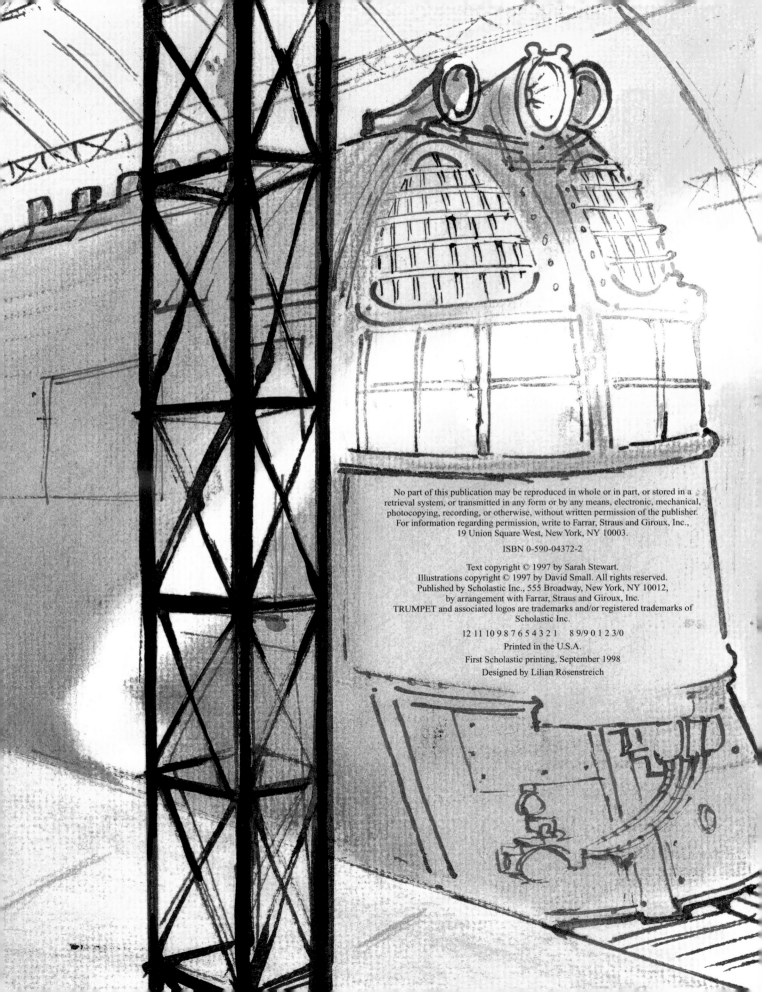

ISBN 0-590-04372-2

Text copyright © 1997 by Sarah Stewart.
Illustrations copyright © 1997 by David Small. All rights reserved.
Published by Scholastic Inc., 555 Broadway, New York, NY 10012,
by arrangement with Farrar, Straus and Giroux, Inc.
TRUMPET and associated logos are trademarks and/or registered trademarks of
Scholastic Inc.

12 11 10 9 8 7 6 5 4 3 2 1   8 9/9 0 1 2 3/0
Printed in the U.S.A.
First Scholastic printing, September 1998
Designed by Lilian Rosenstreich

Sarah Stewart
PICTURES BY David Small